#1

MARVEL

A BLACK PANTHER ADVENTURE

SHURI

PRINCESS

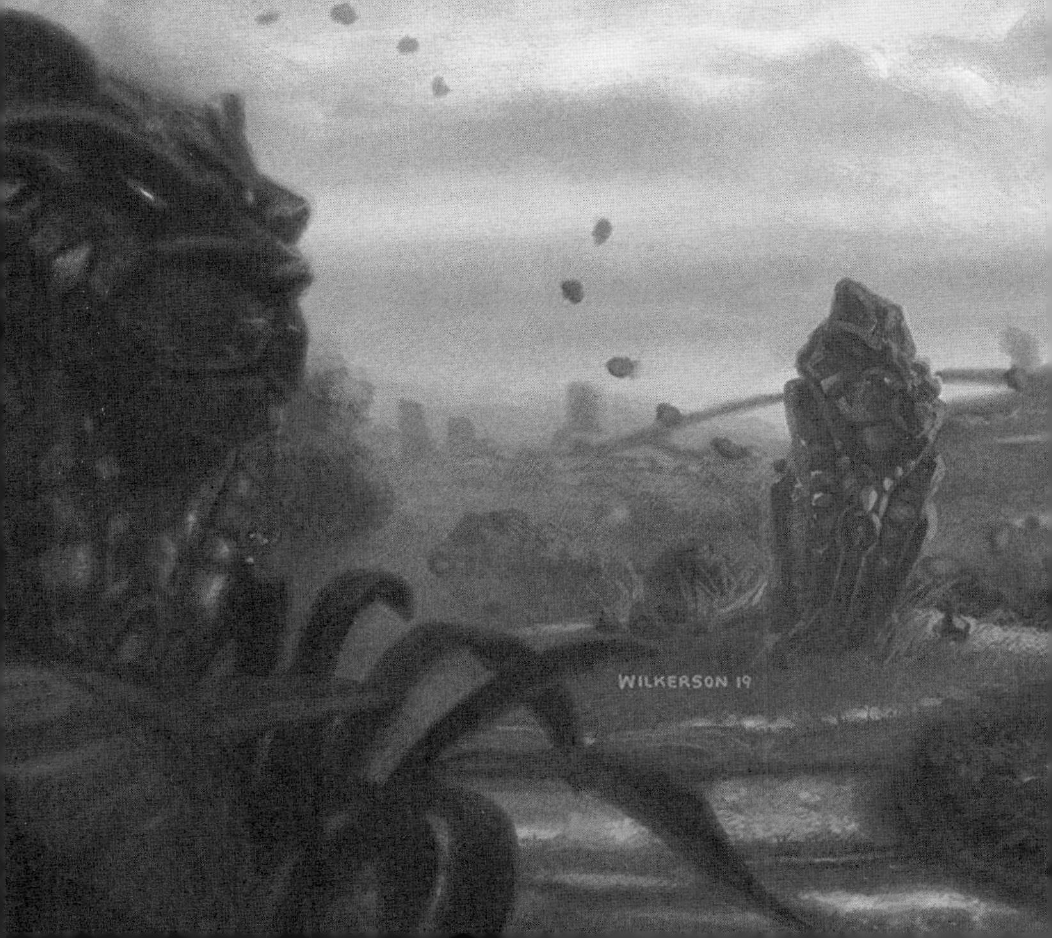

SHURI

BY **NIC STONE**

SCHOLASTIC INC.

ABDOBOOKS.COM

Reinforced library bound edition published in 2021 by Spotlight, a division of ABDO, PO Box 398166, Minneapolis, Minnesota 55439. Spotlight produces high-quality reinforced library bound editions for schools and libraries. Reprinted by permission of Scholastic Inc.

Printed in the United States of America, North Mankato, Minnesota.
092020
012021

THIS BOOK CONTAINS
RECYCLED MATERIALS

© 2020 MARVEL

First printing 2020

Book design by Katie Fitch

Library of Congress Control Number: 2020942437

Publisher's Cataloging-in-Publication Data

Names: Stone, Nic, author.
Title: Princess / by Nic Stone
Description: Minneapolis, Minnesota : Spotlight, 2021. | Series: Shuri: a Black Panther adventure; #1
Summary: Shuri would rather be in her lab than perform her princess duties, but when she learns of rumors of an invasion and that Wakanda's heart-shaped herb plants are dying, she must figure out how to save the plants in time for Challenge Day.
Identifiers: ISBN 9781532147739 (lib. bdg.)
Subjects: LCSH: Shuri (Fictitious character)--Juvenile fiction. | Wakanda (Africa : Imaginary place)--Juvenile fiction. | Princesses--Juvenile fiction. | Plants--Juvenile fiction. | Adventure and adventurers--Juvenile fiction. | Black Panther (Fictitious character)--Juvenile fiction | Graphic novels--Juvenile fiction
Classification: DDC [Fic]--dc23

Spotlight
A Division of ABDO
abdobooks.com

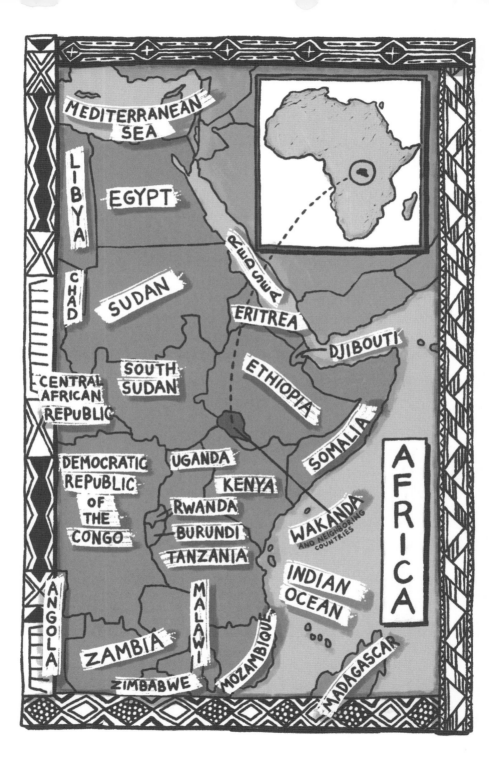

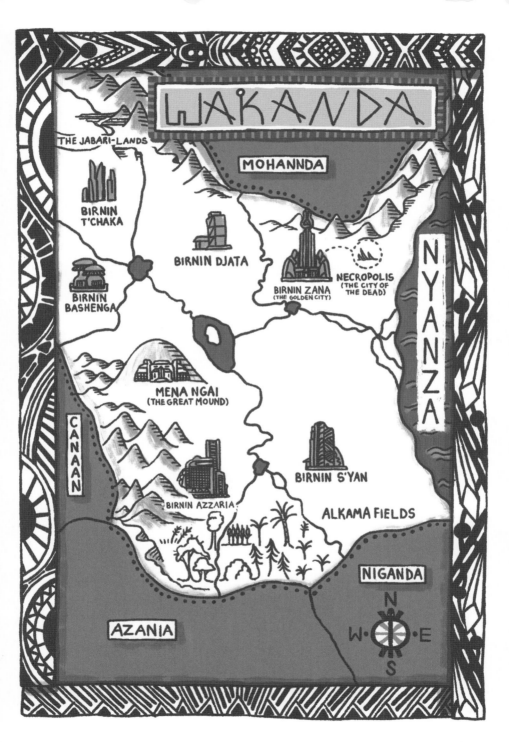

PROLOGUE

S he didn't know she'd have to fight.

"Who are you?" she asks, a feeble effort to keep him talking, though she has no idea what that will accomplish. Perhaps her trio of former Dogs of War will happen to turn the corner at just the right moment to come to her rescue . . .

In fact, if you told her a *fight* would be waiting for her the first time she left Wakanda, she'd roll her dark eyes and wave you off like a conspiracy theory (which has no foundation in science).

"Who I am is of no consequence, Princess. The only thing that truly matters is what I plan to do . . ."

Not that she'd ever admit it aloud, but she's not even sure she *can* fight. Thanks to Mother, she hasn't truly trained in years. She was still a single digit in age the last time she made a fist.

"And what's that?" Shuri carefully, clandestinely shifts her feet into a fighting stance. Because she has a hunch about what his response will be.

Because fight she will.

"Well, to start, I intend to prevent your return to your beloved homeland."

For herself. Her life.

Her future.

For her people. For *their* future.

She will go out of her way. She will risk it all.

Her very existence.

The princess will *fight*.

For Wakanda.

And with that, his hand shoots out quick as a flash, reaching for Shuri's throat . . .

MISSION LOG

THERE IS SOMETHING FISHY GOING ON.

One week ago, my dear brother stormed my lab *begging* me to make him a new Panther Habit. "This one is too restrictive," he said, holding up the form-fitting catsuit he currently wears as our nation's ruler and protector, the Black Panther. "It hasn't been updated since Baba wore it. Can you *please* make me a new one? And fast?"

I could not have been more excited. I would never tell *him* because it would go right to his watermelon head, but I quite enjoy when T'Challa requests my assistance. Our father died when I was very young, but I think he'd be proud to see his only daughter doing her part to keep our nation safe and secure.

And anyway: The current habit *does* make T'Challa's butt look funny.

I scoured the markets for a . . . *stretchier* fabric. Something with an easy-to-manipulate molecular structure that would bond well with my favorite substance and our nation's most valuable resource: Vibranium. In theory, the correct composition will allow T'Challa to kick high and flip fast, but also absorb kinetic energy from any hits he takes, gather it in the palms of his gloves, and shoot it out as sonic blasts (*FWOOM FWOOM*) that will knock opponents right out of their shoes.

Except nothing is working. *Stretchier* apparently means thinner, and none of the existing fabrics I've tried can handle the optimal amount of Vibranium. I've managed to merge two of the trial fabrics into something new—and sufficiently stretchy—but even this hybrid material can only withstand 73 percent of the total volume of the magic metal in the previous habit. This is fine in terms of shock absorption and turning his hands into cannons, but the 17 percent decrease in bodily protection . . . well, I doubt big bro would be okay with punches and kicks hurting *more*.

My original idea was to distill the heart-shaped herb down to its strength-enhancing, speed-increasing, agility-augmenting essence, and infuse it into the fabric. That way, the longer the material is against T'Challa's skin and he's breathing through the mask, the more powerful and panther-like he would be.

However, the distillation process has proved more challenging than I anticipated.

In the first trial, I created a powder and then attempted to work it into the fabric by kneading. Seemed promising at first, but the moment I stretched it out, a puff of the powder filled the air. I inhaled it and . . . fainted. (Apparently those rumors about the herb taking out the unworthy are true. Bast forbid someone *not* of royal blood catches a whiff.

Also, the powder leaves a dusty film on the skin that makes one's skin appear in dire need of moisturization. And there's no way T'Challa would be okay with looking ashy once the suit retracts.)

In trial two, I tried a vapor. Which might've worked had I not put my head over the flask to check it and fainted again.

Trial three? A gel encased in patches as a suit lining. Thought I'd nailed it with this one . . . But then I tried to pull the piece of test fabric from my arm, and let me tell you: Band-Aid adhesive doesn't have a THING on Vibranium gel patches. *OUCH*.

Fourth and current trial *seemed* a step in the right direction: I lined the fabric with tiny liquid-filled bulbs that would break when hit, delivering small amounts of Heart-Shaped essence to the skin at the point of impact.

And it *does* work—I wrapped a piece around the midsection of a mannequin and gave it a good kick. The liquid *does* release at the point of impact, and *will* coat the skin (maybe even enhancing cell regeneration and creating a speed-healing effect that would prevent pain and bruising? Must test this later . . . In fact, there's a good bit I could test later. Which has me wondering if anyone has ever *studied* the herb before).

But it makes my entire lab reek of rotten fish.

And I just used my last herb bulb.

Frosting on the cake? I have a dead-line now. T'Challa just *appeared* in my lab in holographic form—perks of being able to override any and all security protocols, I suppose—to tell me that he needs the new habit by this Friday. That's five days hence.

Guessing he wants it for our ritual Challenge Day. Which would make sense. There's no telling who will come forward to face off against T'Challa for the throne and mantle of Black Panther, and though T'Challa is *virtually unbeatable*, as he likes to claim, an updated suit would certainly be to his advantage.

Come to think of it, our uncle S'Yan—who

stepped in to fill the role of Black Panther after Baba's death—was wearing the current habit when T'Challa challenged *him* four years ago.

And T'Challa obviously won.

No wonder he wants to be rid of the thing.

Back to the drawing board, I guess.

Wakanda forever.

1

PRINCESS

No sooner than Princess Shuri places her mission log Kimoyo bead into its nest for upload, her mother walks in.

And waves her nose.

"My goodness, Shuri, what have you been up to in here?"

"*Mother!*" Shuri exclaims, darting around the room, collecting flasks and vials and odds and ends in a futile attempt to clear some of the chaos. Despite the lab being a sacred space created just for *her* three years ago as a tenth-birthday present from her darling brother, Shuri knows how her mother, in all her queen-liness, feels about messy spaces. Especially work-related ones. "Did you not see the *Experimentation in Progress* sign on the door? You're supposed to ring the bell!"

Queen Ramonda flicks the notion away as if it's little more than a pesky insect buzzing around one of her elaborate head coverings. Shuri often wonders whether her mother's myriad hats, wraps, and scarves put a strain on her neck.

"I'm serious, Mother! What if I'd been . . . testing the effects of gamma radiation on Vibranium or something? You could've been injured!"

"The only thing that could injure me in this place is the turmoil. Or perhaps the *stench*. Have I not told you, a cluttered space is the sign of a—"

"—cluttered mind. Yes, yes. You've been telling me that since the time I used to dismantle Baba's gadgets in my pre-primary years." Shuri grabs the unrolled bolt of shimmering gunmetal fabric that lies draped across two chairs, the shoulders of a mannequin, and a pile of books, and begins to roll it up. Knocking over an open box of circuits and loose wires with a deafening *CRASH* in the process.

Ramonda's fingertips go to her temples. "Beloved ancestors, why do you vex me with this child?"

"You know you love me, Mother!" Shuri says as she trips on a panther boot prototype and goes sprawling. "Oops."

Queen Ramonda sighs. "Yes. I do." She reaches down to pull her daughter to her feet. "Which is precisely why I am here to escort you to the dress fitting I've no doubt you've forgotten about."

Shuri's smile tumbles to the floor, landing somewhere in the pile of fishy-smelling material. "Dress fitting?"

"My point, precisely. Come now."

"Aww, Mother!"

But it's no use, and Shuri knows it. The queen's word is final. So with a huff and longing glance over her shoulder, she trails her mother out of her favorite place on Earth.

All the way to her *least* favorite place: the glorified oversize closet—with bathroom space—that comprises the queen's dressing chambers.

Queen Ramonda was right in assuming that Shuri had forgotten not only about the dress fitting but the reason for it as well.

Now in addition to being grabbed and prodded and turned and poked like a pincushion ("She's just so *wiggly*," Lwazi, the royal clothier, mutters), Shuri is also being treated to a verbal lashing by the queen mother.

"*How* does the princess of a nation—who is first in line to the throne, no less!—forget about the Taifa Ngao as if it means nothing?"

Mother is pacing. Shuri hates it when she paces. "*Relax*, Mother—*eek!*" Shuri shrieks as she's pin-pricked again.

"I will not *relax*. At least one of us has to take things seriously, Shuri. It isn't as if the tribal elders gather frequently. These meetings are vital for the continued unity and well-being of Wakanda! This particular one especially!"

As Shuri now knows—Mother has been walloping her over the head with it since the moment they'd exited Shuri's lab—there's a council meeting this after-noon. It's the final one scheduled before Challenge Day. During *this* meeting, the tribal leaders will dis-cuss security concerns and other Important Matters.

So fine: It's one Shuri probably should have remembered.

That being said, Mother does seem more *vexed*, as she likes to put it, about things than Shuri feels is warranted.

"Mother, is something wrong?" Shuri asks as Lwazi finishes removing her from what feels like a fabric cocoon and begins to pack his pins, needles, and the like.

"Of course not. Why would you ask that?" the queen replies. As the clothier exits the space, she drags Shuri to a velvet-topped stool at the center of the vast room and shoves her down onto it. "Perfect timing on the fitting. The braiders have arrived."

"The braiders?!" Shuri's arms cross over her head. "But why?"

"Tuh! You think I would permit your appearance in front of the elders with *that* mess on top of your head?"

"There's nothing wrong with my hair!"

"Tell it to the gods," Ramonda replies. "Perhaps they will hear you."

At that moment, three women with luminescent brown skin stride into the room wearing identical bloodred silk robes with matching cylindrical caps. They look, to Shuri, like angels of scalp death. She wishes she had a small vial of heart-shaped herb essence to drop on the floor—there is no doubt the beautiful braiders would all flee from the fishy stench.

"Forgive my impropriety, Mother—"

"I won't have to if you refrain from being improper, Shuri."

The princess huffs. "I was just *thinking*...
T'Challa has promised to make me the minister
of Technology and Advancement in just a few
years' time. Wouldn't *this* time be better spent in
my lab, building and experimenting and discover-
ing new uses for our beloved Vibranium instead of
these—*OW!*—relatively...*impractical* aesthetic
pursuits? *OUCH!*"

"If the princess would not mind holding *still*..."
the braider on Shuri's right side says. They have her
surrounded: one on the left, one on the right, one at
Shuri's back, and Mother standing sentinel in front
with what Shuri knows are wildly bejeweled hands
clasped behind her.

"Even as minister of Computers and Progress—"

"*Technology* and *Advancement*." (*Oh, to have a
mother who takes my passions so seriously*, Shuri
thinks.)

"Yes, that. Even with *that* role, you will still be the
sole princess of this nation, Shuri. You are a *royal*. Bast
chose to bestow upon *your* ancestor the mantles of
ruler and Black Panther. Looking the part is an ines-
capable aspect of the position."

"But Mother—"

"Don't *but Mother* me, Shuri."

"This *hurts!*"

The queen bends at the waist so she and Shuri are eye-to-eye. "The pain is temporary, my dear." She takes Shuri's arms at the wrist and crosses them over her chest to form an X. "But Wakanda is forever."

As the braiders continue their torture, Shuri's eyes roam the chamber. Above the wall of lighted mirrors in front of her are painted portraits of Wakanda's queens, present and past. Ramonda's is there. Shuri remembers bursting into the room where her mother was perched—with perfect posture—on a tufted, red velvet chair edged in gold. The princess was six years old at most and wanted to show her mother her latest creation: a drone with a Vibranium-centric flight mechanism that used sound waves to stay airborne. The louder the noise, the closer the thing would fly to it.

Which the painter found out the hard way. "OUT THIS INSTANT!" he boomed. And the drone flew right into the still-wet nose of Mother's portrait.

Shuri smiles at the memory, but as her eyes dance over the other queens—everyone is there, from her father's mother to that grandmother's grandmother's grandmother—a little well of disquiet opens up inside her.

Her gaze sticks on N'Yami, T'Challa's birth mother. The woman passed away long before Shuri was born, but Shuri knows that before she married T'Chaka, Shuri and T'Challa's father, N'Yami was the chief scientist of Wakanda.

Did N'Yami step away from her scientific pursuits when she became queen? Did she shirk her lab gear for fancy dresses and glittering jewelry and elaborate headwear?

What about the other queens? Did they have endeavors beyond occupying the throne? It's not that Shuri believes her mother's job is frivolous—she's fully aware of the mental and emotional fortitude necessary to spearhead diplomacy for an entire nation, even one that remains hidden from the world at large.

But what else were queens permitted to actually *do*?

And what of the other princesses? There certainly was no tribute to them anywhere. At least not one Shuri's seen or heard of. How many of the queens looking out over this most *queenly* of rooms in the royal palace birthed daughters?

Had any of *those* princesses been scientists? Tinkerers? Builders of drones with Vibranium flight mechanisms? Clearly their brothers ascended to the throne and took wives, and those wives are the ones featured in these portraits . . . but what of the royal daughters?

Shuri is snatched back into the present as the braider on the left rips through a clump of tangled coils with a fine-toothed comb ("Weapons of mass destruction, those things," she once complained to her mother). The women above her are chattering about Challenge Day. "Do you think anyone will come forward?" one is asking.

"To face T'Challa?" another replies. "They'd have to be mad."

"Agreed. T'Challa is the fiercest Black Panther Wakanda has ever seen."

But the same was said of Baba, and we see what happened to him.

The thought arises in Shuri's head unbidden, surprising her with its sharpness. Its *truth*.

An image of T'Challa holding Baba's Panther Habit in his hand floats before Shuri's eyes.

She blinks it away and returns her focus to the portraits.

Whether or not those women—or their daughters—had active roles in keeping Wakanda safe, Shuri doesn't know.

But she does know one thing: T'Challa requested *her* help.

She has to figure out that habit.

2

COUNCIL

The only thing Shuri hates more than Taifa Ngao meetings is having to wear a dress.

Which means today is a day most blessed for the princess: She's being treated to both.

Due to some strange sewing sorcery, by the end of Shuri's two-hour braiding session this morning, the clothier had returned with a frock draped over his arm that shifted from blue to green to purple, like beetle wings, based on how the light hit it.

The fabric was certainly beautiful—it made Shuri wish she'd been wearing her microscope goggles so she could've examined its molecular structure—but *wearing* the thing was wildly uncomfortable. T'Challa had taught her to be ready for the unexpected, but dresses always required extra work for full maneuverability.

At least it has pockets.

"Stand up straight," the queen mother says as she and Shuri wait outside the doors to the throne room, flanked by Okoye and Nakia, the two Dora Milaje Shuri admires most. (*Why are there no portraits of them in a place of honor?* Shuri wonders. Considering how long the warrior women have been guarding the royal family, it feels like quite the travesty.) Ramonda pushes a knuckle into the divot between two of her daughter's vertebrae in just the right spot to make Shuri's shoulder blades snap together, drawing her up to attention.

"OW!" Shuri cries.

"Much better."

Okoye coughs, clearly to cover a laugh, and the retort that forms on Shuri's tongue is so bitter, she's relieved when the doors begin to open and she's forced to swallow it down.

It's a relief that doesn't last. Because as Shuri takes in the upturned noses and puckered pouts of the tribal elders, who are already seated in the overwrought chairs brought in specifically for these dumb council meetings and arranged in a semicircle with T'Challa's throne at the head, she'd like nothing more than to lift her oddly asymmetrical skirts and *run*.

Her stomach roils and she passes gas instead.

Of course everyone hears it.

"Shuri!" her mother furiously whispers.

"Sorry! It slipped!"

Pulling her*self* together, Queen Ramonda forces a smile.

But then she grabs on to Shuri's arm just above the elbow. And Shuri can feel the dampness of her mother's palm and the slight tremor in her hand.

Something's not right. Shuri's certain of it now.

Also: Where is T'Challa?

"Beloved leaders!" Ramonda purrs in the liquid silk voice she turns on when it's time to remind everyone who's queen.

And it works. Like magic, the storm cloud of tension permeating the space—and causing all the elders to appear as though they are sucking on sour candies (or maybe that's from Shuri's flatulence)—dissipates like a vapor. Even Shuri's shoulders relax a bit. Though she does draw them back up tight to avoid another knuckle poke.

Shuri's 98.3 percent sure she could *never* have that effect on a room full of Very Important (old) People.

"Thank you all so very much for being here with us today," the queen continues as she guides Shuri forward so the two of them can take their seats, Ramonda to the chair that would put her on T'Challa's left, and Shuri to the one on the right. "As you all know, this is our final gathering prior to Challenge Day—"

"Where is T'Challa?"

The question comes from a woman who looks *elder* enough to have been around when Bast chose the first-ever Black Panther. She can't remember the woman's name—or *any* of their names other than Eldress Umbusi, head of the Mining Tribe—but Shuri's pretty sure the lady is of the Merchant Tribe.

No wonder her people are known for being *shrewd* in their business dealings. Clearly, they get right to the point.

The question hangs in the air for a moment and then:

"T'Challa sends his apologies for his absence. He's been called to attend to a rather time-sensitive matter. He did request that I assure all of you of his *readiness* for the impending Challenge."

"Oy, brother. Bigheaded even in absence—" The words have launched off the princess's too-quick tongue before she even realizes they've formed. And the silence that follows them into what suddenly feels like a defiled sacred space—what with T'Challa's chair empty—makes Shuri feel as though a bucket of Vibranium-infused ice water has been poured over her freshly braided head.

But then a man—leader of the Border Tribe if the rhinoceros-head hat is any indication—guffaws. And bursts into laughter. "The girl has a point, eh? Our young king is most certainly not lacking in confidence."

"So very true!" Umbusi chimes in. Now everyone in the room is laughing.

"Perhaps," Ramonda replies. "But it would still do the *princess* well not to speak ill of our king when he is not present to defend himself." She's smiling as well. Which makes Shuri feel better than she'd be willing to admit. "Now if we could move ahead to the reason for our gathering today. I'm sure you all have pressing issues outside the capital that you stepped away from to be here, so we'll keep it brief."

"Hear, hear," crows the River Tribe elder. His loose, shimmery blue clothing flows like water. Which is a bit on the nose if you ask Shuri.

"Per usual, there is no representative here among us from the Jabari-Lands. They remain distant, but peaceful as far as we know, holding to their cultural and religious traditions and continuing to reject our technological advancements."

"Fools," from the Merchant eldress, again wasting no time and pulling no punches.

Not that Shuri disagrees with her. The idea of someone actively *avoiding* technology, and the joy of experimentation that comes with seeking to master it, is further beyond her than pulling off this whole "princess" gig.

"We shall respect our brethren and their chosen way of life so long as it does not interfere with the safety of Wakanda."

"They don't even communicate with *us*," Umbusi says, flicking away any notion of Jabari treachery. "What means of contact would they have with the outside world? The Jabari are harmless. Let us leave them be."

"My thoughts precisely, Eldress," Queen Ramonda replies.

"But what do they *do* up there?" The head of the Border Tribe looks concerned. "What if they are stockpiling resources and building weapons for an eventual revolt?"

"Been watching American films on the PantherTube again, eh, old man?" the River Tribe head says, chiding his friend. Everyone chuckles.

"Perhaps this will be the year they send down a challenger," the Merchant eldress says. "Can T'Challa truly prepare for something he has never seen?"

"I do believe he can," from the queen mother.

Shuri gulps, nervous about speaking up, but struggling to resist the compulsion to defend her brother, especially after her earlier bumble. "As do I. It is part and parcel to the Panther mantle to be ready for anything—"

"Except for the Taifa Ngao." The words are sharp-edged as they pass through the Border Tribe elder's lips, but to Shuri's relief, everyone chuckles. The queen's laughter is forced, Shuri can tell, but it works to temper what could very easily become a diplomacy nightmare. Shuri's fairly sure a ruler skipping out on a meeting with his advisory council would be frowned upon in *any* nation.

"Speaking of the Challenge—"

Another area where the queen mother excels and Shuri falters: regaining control of a conversation.

"—if any of you have warriors who intend to challenge T'Challa for the Black Panther mantle *and* the throne, do remind him of the rules: honorable hand-to-hand combat, no specialized weapons or tactics permitted. And should he succeed in besting our present ruler and protector, ingesting the heart-shaped herb to prove himself worthy, and receiving the blessing of Bast, will still be required of him."

"Or her," Shuri murmurs under her breath.

"What was that, young lady?" the Merchant Tribe eldress says. (No filter *and* supersonic hearing? Maybe *she* should be the Black Panther.)

Despite having no idea *why* she said it in the first place, Shuri takes a deep breath and repeats herself. "I just said, 'or *her*.'" And she shoves down her inclination to leave it at that. "Because perhaps a female warrior will step forward to challenge."

Now everyone is *really* laughing. Which makes Shuri feel not only angry and stupid, but also powerless.

"Child, the last warrior to challenge a sitting Black Panther was your brother. And after the way he pommeled your uncle S'yan, not a single male warrior in all of Wakanda has had the courage to face him," the Border Tribe elder says. "Our best and brightest female warriors *serve* the Black Panther as Dora Milaje. They don't try to become him."

Shuri's gaze floats to Okoye and Nakia, who are standing sentinel near the doors. If they're bothered by the older man's words, it doesn't show.

This is why she despises these meetings. In addition to being mind-numbingly boring, all these people insist on treating her like a little girl. Shuri is young, yes, but she has certainly contributed to the well-being of Wakanda. Not a single person in the room outside of her mother ever even refers to Shuri as "princess."

Also, it gives her pause that *these* people can't even seem to fathom a female Black Panther. What rhino-head elder said is certainly true: The Dora Milaje have served as Wakanda's royal guard for ages. And they're the best of the best.

Shuri's mind drifts back to the queen's dressing chamber. The lack of tribute to Wakandan princesses. It makes her wonder: Why has there never been a female Black Panther?

"What of the invasion rumors, Ramonda?" The Merchant eldress strikes again. The more Shuri looks at her, the more her bloodred caftan, black jewelry, and pointed hat seem wildly appropriate.

She's certainly got everyone's attention now.

"Invasion?" from Umbusi. "Is this the true reason T'Challa is not with us?"

This time when Shuri glances at her mother, the queen is looking back at her, but quickly averts her eyes.

It feels foreboding.

"I can assure all of you there is nothing to worry about," the queen replies. "Not even the slightest hint of reason for alarm."

No one seems convinced.

"There will be no invasion, so let us lay that rumor to rest," she continues. "Challenge Day shall proceed as normal, and after it has passed, we shall resume our planning for increased fortification—"

"If there won't be an invasion, what need do we have to fortify?" A valid question from the River Tribe elder, though Shuri is irritated at *his* "impropriety" in interrupting the queen.

"Well . . ." Ramonda clears her throat. Which is something she *never* does. No matter how nervous or uncomfortable Mother gets, it never shows. She is the grand mistress of schooled features and an excellent bluff face. Shuri knows *this* from years of mistakingly playing an American game called Uno that T'Challa had brought back from a surveillance jaunt in a city called New Jersey. (What happened to *Old* Jersey, the princess doesn't know.)

"T'Challa should really be the person to tell you all," the queen goes on.

"But you are here and so are we," says Umbusi. "The next Taifa Ngao is four months hence. Wakanda is surely the *most* fortified nation on the planet. We've remained hidden—and therefore *un*invaded, unconquered, and uncolonized—for the entirety of our existence as a nation. If there is need for us to fortify further, all the tribal elders should be privy to *why*."

"Seconded—"

"And thirded," comes the boom of the Border Tribe elder's voice, following that of his River Tribe companion. (Of course the men back one another up.)

The queen mother sighs. "Fine," she says, and everyone seems to pull forward in their cushy seats as if that single word is a magnet.

"I won't say much because it is not my place to speak for the king. But T'Challa has seen and done much during his relatively brief tenure as the ruler and protector of Wakanda, and I believe that, after making our borders as secure as possible, he intends to make our nation's existence a bit less . . . secret."

3

INVADER

Shuri's mind whirls as she makes her way to her quarters after the close of the meeting. All she can think about is . . . Baba. How can T'Challa even *consider* making their existence known to the world? Especially considering what happened.

T'Challa had been just a few months younger than Shuri is now when their father was killed. According to the story she knows, Baba had also considered making the world aware of their small nation. He'd accepted an invitation to some gathering of world leaders, and there was someone there—a man named Klaw—who'd been sent to kill him.

The most troublesome part to the princess: Because T'Challa had been so young, Baba's brother, Uncle S'Yan, had assumed the throne and taken on the Black Panther mantle until T'Challa reached the point where he could challenge him for it.

Shuri is the only other living descendant of T'Chaka. Which would mean if something were to happen to T'Challa, *she* would have to step up. There's never been a female Black Panther before, but what if there has to be? What if . . . it has to be Shuri?

So distracted by these thoughts is the princess, she doesn't realize there is someone in her quarters until she's all the way inside with the door shut.

"*Finally*, you're back!" a girl's (Shuri thinks) voice says. "I was beginning to wonder if I needed to convene a search party."

Quick as a flash, Shuri whips around and extends her arm, palm up, as she makes a fist and lets her hand drop just the slightest bit. A blast of purple light—and electromagnetic energy, though the intruder won't know that until it hits them—shoots out of the bead at the center of her Kimoyo bracelet, and she drops and rolls forward so that she's hidden behind her giant bed.

"What the—OWW!" the voice says. "Uncalled for!"

It makes the princess smile. She'd gotten the idea to arm that bead from a video of a guy who swings around New York City on webbing he shoots from his wrists. *Thank you, spidery guy*, she thinks—

But then there's movement above her—a bounce on the bed—and the next thing Shuri knows, a pair of arms are wrapping around her from behind, one at the neck, and one around the chest, pinning her arms.

Shuri thrashes . . . well, she *tries* to, at least. The person is very strong, and Shuri's too out of practice for her twists and turns to do much of anything.

Though she has to admit: The invader seems shorter than she would've expected.

"A little rusty, eh?" the voice purrs in her ear.

"Let me go!" Shuri barks.

"As you wish . . ." The arms release her, and faster than she can blink, the person has slipped in front of Shuri, grabbed her pulse-shooting arm, and flipped her onto her back on the bed.

A girl's face appears above the princess. Round, deep brown, and set with dark eyes that now sparkle with mischief. "By Bast, you are *dramatic*," she says. "Shooting at me? Really?"

"Oh," Shuri says, the fight going out of her. "It's you." She sits up.

The girl puts her hands on her hips—which are clad in violently bright orange-and-pink patterned trousers. "Well, don't sound so excited!" She's a full head shorter than Shuri, but with athletic curves and muscles the princess is severely lacking. "I'm only your *best* friend in the whole wide world—who's been waiting here for an *hour*, by the way, and who you haven't seen in *ages*—come to invite you on a grand adventure! No big deal at all!"

And she calls *Shuri* "dramatic."

"I saw you two days ago, K'Marah." Her pride crushed, Shuri stands and shucks off the green, toe-squishing, Achilles-pinching contraptions the clothier delivered with her fancy frock. Then she crosses the cool, marble floor to her dressing chamber. She wants *out* of this dress—and away from both the girl and her own embarrassment at being trounced so thoroughly. "And knowing you, whatever 'adventure' you have in mind will be something I want no parts of."

I really want no parts of this so-called friendship, Shuri wants to say, but doesn't. Not that friendship itself is something she shuns . . . not that she'd ever admit it aloud, but the inside jokes and shared fun Shuri has witnessed between girls her and K'Marah's age would be nice from time to time. (Bonus if there's an opportunity to talk science and tech.)

It's just that Shuri's friendship with K'Marah has never felt *real*.

While T'Challa's tenth-birthday gift to Shuri was a laboratory near the Sacred Mound, and access to as much Vibranium as she needs for her technological pursuits, Queen Ramonda's gift to her daughter was a *friend*. "You spend far too much time alone, child," she'd said. "People are beginning to ask questions." (Shuri thought *people* should mind their own business, but of course she didn't say that, either.)

In theory, an arranged friendship isn't *such* a bad thing, especially if the friends genuinely like each other and enjoy each other's company. And it's not that Shuri *dis*likes K'Marah or is *opposed* to her presence. She's just never been fully able to lower her guard.

For one: K'Marah is Eldress Umbusi's granddaughter. Could it be mere coincidence that the princess was given unlimited access to Vibranium—Wakanda's most valuable resource, yes, but also the main item in the Mining Tribe's jurisdiction—on the same day Mother introduced her to the short, pretty girl whose position within the Mining Tribe is akin to Shuri's position in the Wakandan royal family?

Maybe.

But last year when K'Marah began training to become a Dora Milaje, Shuri began to seriously doubt it. (She may also have been a bit jealous, but that's neither here nor there.)

In truth, it's not just the princess-and-princess-protector-in-training nature of the relationship that makes Shuri uncomfortable. She and K'Marah are just so . . . different. Shuri is tall and slim, and hates drawing attention to herself—hence her preference for simple T-shirts and slacks. K'Marah, as evidenced by her neon pants and ruffled tank top, is the opposite.

Also: Where Shuri is grounded, logical, a lover of science, technology, and empiricism, K'Marah thinks more loftily, preferring the "spiritual," as she calls it: the *intangible* and *ethereal*.

Which is precisely why Shuri has no interest in any "adventure" her so-called friend wants to partake in. In fact, the last time the princess allowed the Mining heiress to rope her into an escapade—K'Marah had met some self-proclaimed "spirit scientist" in the market who'd shared a "foolproof" way (using self-hypnosis, which she didn't realize was a thing) to incorporeally project oneself straight onto the Djalia, the plane of Wakandan memory where one can commune with the spirits of the ancestors—Shuri wound up unconscious for six hours, and woke with a splitting headache that required a trip to the royal healers.

"That dress is really stunning, by the way!" K'Marah calls out just as Shuri lets it fall to the floor within her closet space. "The color really makes your melanin pop!"

Shuri rolls her eyes as K'Marah's latest obsession with aesthetics comes to the fore. "Been watching beauty guru videos on PantherTube again, eh?" she shouts.

"I know it's not really your thing, but there's one hair tutorial you *must* watch. I'll send it to your Kimoyo card—"

At the mention of the Wakandan gadget (akin to a "smartphone," as she's heard them called on the internet, but thinner, virtually indestructible, and *far* technologically superior), Shuri's mind drifts off to one of her recent projects: a pair of eyeglasses embedded with the card's technology. The CatEyes will be fully communicative—one can make calls, send/receive messages, etc.—AND will give the wearer instant access to any information a Wakandan could need with the mere tap of a finger. Just the thought sends an excited thrill down Shuri's spine.

"There. I sent." K'Marah has appeared in the doorway of Shuri's dressing chamber with her own Kimoyo card in hand.

Except Shuri's been off in what the queen mother calls "intellectual la-la land" . . . which means she hasn't gotten dressed.

"Do you *mind*?" she says to K'Marah, ducking behind the mannequin.

(Yes, there's a mannequin in Shuri's closet. As well as a fold-down experimentation station that is presently tucked into the wall. Mother forbids Shuri to spend *all* her waking hours in her lab, so the princess had to improvise. Eureka moments wait for no one.)

"Oh pish posh," K'Marah replies with a wave of her hand and a roll of her eyes. "It's not as though you have anything to *see*." And she walks out.

Despite the sting of the comment, Shuri is thrown back to the Taifa Ngao and the thought of Wakanda's exposure. Because one thing's for sure: While Shuri might be shaped like the River Tribe elder's walking stick, there's definitely plenty in Wakanda to *see*.

And *steal* if you let the head of the Border Tribe tell it.

He was outraged at the very *idea* of Wakanda's existence being revealed to the rest of the world. He spat phrases like *invitation to colonizers* and *pillage of resources* and *utter razing of our land* at the queen mother like poisonous darts. Never had Shuri been more aware of the empty throne at the center of the room.

And never had she been more afraid for her brother—and her homeland.

Another dissenter? That was K'Marah's beloved grandmother.

"K'Marah, may I ask you something?" Shuri asks as she steps back into her bedroom. The other girl is now lying belly-down on the four-poster bed, flipping through Shuri's old textbook on particle physics. Which is missing from the bedside table.

"You just did," K'Marah replies without looking up. "How can you stand to *read* this dreck? It looks like an alien language."

"I'm serious." The princess pulls the book from K'Marah's grip and shuts it with a snap before rolling K'Marah over like a log and taking a seat on the bed beside her. "You've invaded my space. Might as well make yourself useful."

"Well, tell me how you *really* feel, Princess."

"Do you think it would be bad if we weren't hidden?" Shuri continues, ignoring the sarcasm.

"Last I checked, you hide by choice. Which is probably good considering your severe lack of *panache* and tiresome insistence upon 'empiricalism,' or whatever you call it. You could stand to lighten up a bit."

"*Empiricism*," Shuri huffs. "And that's not what I meant."

"So what do you mean?" K'Marah drags herself over to the edge of the bed and sits up so she and Shuri are side by side.

"Our nation. We've been hidden for centuries. Never invaded. Never conquered. Wholly independent. What do you think would happen if other nations knew about us?"

"Other nations *do* know about us, Shuri."

Panic. "What do you mean?"

K'Marah looks at Shuri as though she just asked for the definition of a molecule. "You are aware that we are *landlocked*?"

"Umm . . . yes?"

"And that *landlocked* means 'surrounded by land'? And that the land we're surrounded by is broken up into other nations?"

"Yes . . ."

"Are you under the impression that those nations are unaware of our *landlocked* position between them?"

Shuri doesn't respond this time, but she does see her "friend's" point.

Now K'Marah falls back. "If you *are* under that impression, I can assure you: T'Challa attends every gathering of the Pan-African Congress. And based on some of the stuff he said at the most recent one—"

"You were *there*?"

"Mm-hmm. I've been to two so far. Part of my Dora Milaje training. Anyway, I'm pretty sure your dear brother *wants* more people to know about us."

Shuri's so shaken by K'Marah knowing this first-hand, she can hardly form words. "But what about colonizers? Pillagers? Those who would seek to do us harm?!" There's plenty Shuri doesn't know, but one thing she does: Her father's killer wanted Vibranium.

"I'm not sure the world is as awful as you think, Princess. From what I've seen, the ruler of Narobia is a little off, but no one who knows about us thus far seems to wish us ill. Besides, I'm sure everyone will find out about us eventually. Nothing stays hidden in the age of the internet. Now if you don't mind, I'd love to get to my *reason* for being in your quarters."

Shuri sighs, knowing she's not going to get any further with her personal royal-guard-in-training. And K'Marah's right, isn't she? It likely *is* only a matter of time before they're discovered. Perhaps this is something preemptive on T'Challa's part.

Where is her darling brother? And what could he possibly be doing?

"So are you ready to hear where we're going on our quest?" K'Marah says, clearly oblivious to the magnitude of Shuri's distress.

"I'm not going on any quest."

"Fantastic!" K'Marah sits up and scoots close to Shuri so their sides are flush. The excitement radiating off the shorter girl is so palpable, it makes the tiny hairs on Shuri's arms stand at attention.

Shuri hates it, but now she *has* to know what's going on. "Well?" she asks.

"Ha! Knew you'd come around," the other girl says. Then she drops her voice to a whisper. "We're going to sneak down to the bonfire."

"The what?" Shuri asks.

K'Marah puts her head in her hands. "Bast forgive her on *my* behalf."

"Oh, just get on with it," Shuri says, giving her friend a shove.

"It will never cease to amaze me how little the *princess* of this nation seems to care about our traditions."

"You sound like my mother now."

"Once a year there is a ritual bonfire near the baobab tree, and it is said that while the fire burns, a pathway to the Djalia is opened and the spirits of the ancestors will come down to commune with anyone who seeks their wisdom and guidance."

"Wonder if they can tell me how to fix T'Challa's suit," Shuri mumbles irreverently.

"Huh?"

"Nothing. I won't—" But just before Shuri can get "be doing that" out of her mouth, it occurs to her that accompanying K'Marah to the baobab tree will put her in the perfect position to make a visit to the Sacred Field—the only place in Wakanda where the heart-shaped herb grows—without Mother's knowledge. She needs more bulbs and leaves.

"Okay," Shuri says. "When do we leave?"

4

BROKENHEARTED

Within two minutes of reaching the bonfire, Shuri regrets her decision to come. She and K'Marah are both in disguise—in addition to being the Mining heiress, K'Marah is also the niece of the clothier, which means unlimited access to the royal garment repository. But the fear of being spotted isn't as easy to shed as the clothes will be once the princess returns to the palace.

The air is hazy with what amounts to more vapor than smoke. Shuri can feel the difference in the moist coating on her skin and in the way the spicy-sweet scented substance feels inside her nose. She has no idea what substance is at the center of the blaze licking up from a large crater in the landscape some hundred meters from the baobab tree, but she is *sure* nothing organic—nothing of this world even—could cause *this* mist when burned. It makes her spine tingle.

"Perhaps we should go," Shuri says under her breath to K'Marah as a woman cloaked in serpentine green cloth passes by, shaking a collection of gourds and what look like . . . bones. On strings. "This was maybe a bad idea—"

"Where is your sense of adventure, O Royal One?"

"Don't *call* me that here! Mother will rake me over the holy coals if it gets back to her that I left the palace with no guard!"

"I *am* your guard."

"Not yet, you aren't!"

K'Marah rolls her eyes, but as they continue toward the fire—and into thicker crowds—even she looks more alert. If Shuri didn't know better, she'd say her dear "friend" is looking for someone. "Don't tell me you have a rendezvous planned . . ." the princess says. "K'Marah, I swear to the gods—"

"No, no, nothing like that." The shorter girl rises to her toes (like that helps) and cups a hand over her brow, squinting. She turns her gaze skyward before shifting to look in a different direction, then she jumps once (which does help . . . *Girl's got hops*, Shuri thinks, tugging on a phrase she once heard T'Challa say while watching something called basketball). "Nothing like that at all. Come, let's get closer."

The heat rises as they near the blaze, but Shuri has a sinking suspicion that the increase in temperature has more to do with the increase in bodies wrapped in thick fabrics than with the fire itself. In fact, as she sticks a hand into the air, it feels cooler.

The girls reach an open space and stop. Shuri has to admit, the sparkle, flicker, and dance of the bright orange flames against the ink-dark sky is entrancing.

For a moment, at least.

Doesn't take long for the princess to realize the pungency and harshness of woodsmoke are completely absent from the atmosphere, and as she ponders over the nature of *actual* fire—the combustion-based chemical reaction that permanently alters the molecular composition of whatever's burning—she becomes more and more convinced that *this* fire is . . . scientifically unsound.

"K'Marah, what exactly are they burni—?"

"Shhhh." The other girl, who, despite the grandmotherly frock and hooded cape she decided to wear, looks just like that—a girl—is standing to Shuri's right with head tilted back and arms slightly aloft, palms up. "The plane is open, and the ancestors are near. Close your eyes and lower your guard so you can feel them."

No, thanks, Shuri thinks but doesn't say. And besides, she couldn't close her eyes if she tried. They're too busy darting around, struggling to process everything she's seeing: the U-shaped arrangement of male drummers, all shirtless, but with intricately painted designs all over their chests and arms; the assortment of dancers, some solo, some in groups, all in varying states of bliss; the smattering of individuals either kneeling or prostrate in prayer.

Beyond the bonfire, the baobab tree looks lit from within, and Shuri could swear there are dark shapes, lounging it seems, in the high branches.

A flicker of blue pulls Shuri's gaze to the flames. Then a tongue of green licks up to her right before a swirl of red begins to spin and twist and dance deep within the blaze. And she feels pulled toward it. The only thing keeping her sandal-clad feet rooted in place is the tenuous grip she's able to maintain on *reason*.

"K'Marah, do you see that?"

But the voice that responds doesn't belong to Shuri's friend. Nor does it come from K'Marah's mouth. In fact, Shuri has no idea where the whispers of *"Uya kuvuka*" and "*Sisindisiwe*" are coming from. She does know that their meanings—*She will rise; We are saved*—would be alarming if not for the fact that they feel like sighs of what must be Earth's most pleasant wind breezing over her skin, even *beneath* the dense tunic, pants, and cloak she's wearing.

But then the red flare begins to move. In Shuri's direction.

She blinks, hoping that what she's seeing isn't real, but that just seems to increase the speed of the mysterious light. There are images forming within it now, nebulous at first, but then condensing into what looks like the torso of a woman holding a globe. The whispers shift, and the wind becomes icy: "*Khusela, khusela . . .*" the voice—*voices* now—cry out. *Protect, protect.* Louder and louder, as the red leaps, now panther-shaped, from within the fire and wraps itself around the princess so tightly, it becomes difficult to draw breath.

Shuri's head swims as the smell and feel of *true* smoke—the dry, toxic kind that irritates the airways and prevents the transfer of oxygen to the blood—overtake her senses.

Then everything goes black.

Shuri is hot. Unbearably so. Her mouth is dry, and as she inhales, the air feels so much like sandpaper against the delicate tissues of her throat and windpipe, she wonders if it's better to just not breathe. Something sharp runs over her cheek, and her eyelids snap open . . .

Though she immediately wishes she could shut them again. There in front of her is a woman. Red-eyed and dry-lipped. Dry-*everything*, in fact: The woman's skin is so lacking in moisture, Shuri can see tiny fault lines where it's begun to crack. Like the drought-wrecked landscapes she's seen in her environmental science digital textbook.

The woman lifts a hand, and the globe Shuri noticed before floats above her palm, seemingly lit from within. And speaking of *within*, the more Shuri stares at the glowing orb, the more she recognizes what's inside it: her homeland.

"What . . . what are you doing?" Panic claws its way up the inside of Shuri's chest, more painful than the dry air going down.

And it's warranted. Because the moment the princess looks into her enemy's (she's sure of it) crimson gaze, the woman smiles, revealing jagged teeth, some of which fall from her head as the princess stares, and squeezes her hand shut, crushing the globe—and Wakanda within it—to dust.

Shuri opens her mouth to scream, and cold air rushes down into her lungs.

"Princess Shuri?"

A male voice.

"What are you doing here?"

Laced with panic.

"Does the queen mother know you've come?"

The space comes into focus around her as her vision adjusts to the darkness. In front of her stands a bald man draped in dark fabric, and leaning on a staff carved to resemble a thick vine.

As Shuri realizes where she is—the veiled entrance to the Sacred Field—the priest peeks over his shoulder and turns back to her.

He's petrified.

"You saw her, too?" Shuri asks, too shaken to even wonder how she got here from the bonfire. Though now that she thinks of it—

"Saw who? Did you bring someone else?"

Now he *really* looks scared.

Something's not right . . .

"Are you all right, Priest . . . ?"

"Kufihli." He bows. "At your service, Your Highness."

"Do you . . ." Now Shuri's the nervous one. "Uhh . . . know how I arrived?"

His brow furrows. "I am not sure I understand what you mean?"

How to ask without sounding as though I've lost all of my Kimoyo beads? "Have I been . . . standing here? For very long, Priest Kufihli?"

"Oh no, no! We would not keep the princess waiting! I came as soon as I heard your approach." He takes another worried glance behind him.

So she *walked* here while in the thick of her vision? And where is K'Marah?

Also: Why is the priest beginning to sweat?

"Is something the matter?" Shuri says, attempting to look past him. When he steps to block her view, she *knows* something's up.

She also knows she's dealt with enough unknowns tonight to last her a lifetime. "I need to grab some bulbs and leaves of the herb to run some tests—"

"NO!" He throws his hands up.

"Excuse me?" The statement flows out of genuine bewilderment, but the priest takes it as an assertion of authority.

"I . . . I am sorry, Your Highness," he says with a bow. "I mean you no disrespect. It is just that . . . ahhh . . ." Another wary look backward. "This is not the best time. Perhaps you can return—"

"No, I cannot." *Not without Mother finding out . . .* Which reminds her to get an oath from him that he won't mention her little visit to anyone. "I must gather the supplies now."

And she pushes past, with him calling "*Wait!*" to her back.

Twenty paces into the tree-shrouded space, she sees why: Half of the Sacred Field is dark, the gently phosphorescent leaves of the heart-shaped herb not only devoid of light, but gray and shriveled.

Dead.

She steps forward, instinctively reaching for one of the desiccated plants.

"Don't!" Priest Kufihli catches Shuri's arm before her hand can make contact. That's when she notices the tiny blooms of yellowish flowers dotting the soil like spores of mold.

"What is *that*?"

"We are unsure, Your Highness. We only know that as the plants die, those blossoms spring up in their place." He gulps then. "Another priest, he . . . well, he fell unconscious very shortly after touching those with his bare hand." He points to the mucus-colored blooms. "He had to be revived by a healer, and he—" Priest Kufihli shudders.

"What? What happened?"

"He almost died, Princess. And he still has not regained use of his right arm."

Shuri is speechless.

"We don't know what is happening, but I can assure you that we are working around the clock to find out—"

"How quickly are the plants dying?"

For a moment, Priest Kufihli is silent. Then he sighs. "At the current rate, the entire field will have withered in approximately five days' time."

"Five days?" Shuri blinks, and the image of the dry woman crushing Wakanda flashes behind her eyes. "But the *Challenge* is in five days! If, Bast forbid, someone bests T'Challa, and needs to partake of the herb to gain the Panther enhancements—"

There won't be any herb left.

And more important: If the herb dies out completely, there won't be any for *Shuri* to consume in the event that she has to take up the mantle.

"I will get to the bottom of this," she says.

MISSION LOG

THIS IS VERY BAD.

Thirty-six hours have elapsed since my return to what *should* be Regularly Scheduled Programming, but after the bizarre events of Bonfire Eve, everything feels upside down, inside out, *and* backward.

I have invested the majority of my physical and cognitive resources into attempts at unraveling the herb issue. I have yet to resume the Panther Habit trials—too scared to waste herb juice—but after countless hours of testing and experimentation, I feel further from understanding the root (no pun intended) of the problem than I was when I first discovered it.

Which seems to be the case with everything pertaining to that night.

What I know for sure:

1. I had what I suppose was a "vision" (*scientific unsoundness duly noted*) near the bonfire. Whether it was a prophecy or some sort of waking nightmare, I am unsure, but when I regained lucidity, I had traveled three-quarters of a kilometer and arrived at the hidden entrance to the Sacred Field.

2. After making my way past a reluctant priest, I discovered an estimated 44 percent of the heart-shaped herb plants in the field utterly decimated by an unknown cause. The dead plants were surrounded by tiny yellow blossoms that impact the functioning of the central nervous system when touched.

3. Upon *exiting* the Sacred Field, I discovered a glaze-eyed K'Marah staring up at the stars. Waiting for me. When I asked her what she was

doing there, she told me that before leaving the fire, I instructed her to meet me just outside the entrance to the field at precisely twenty-two hundred hours.

It was 22:03.

Since our confusing—for me, at least—return to the palace, I have done my best to focus on that which I can control: namely, the herb issue. But every attempt to replant/transplant/dissect/revive the mysterious shrub has resulted in failure.

The liquid essence spoils at precisely the six-hour mark—hello, fishy fragrance!—unless I combine it with something that renders it unconsumable (like foaming hand sanitizer or dish soap, bizarrely enough). I tried encapsulation of both liquid and powdered forms . . . a sort of heart-shaped-herbal pill that isn't shaped like a heart. Sadly, whatever Bast- and/or Vibranium-derived juju that makes the plants so special doesn't play nice with collagen, gelatin, or glycerin:

I wound up with a goopy, burnt-smelling mess that was *very* difficult to get off my hands.

Tried transplanting to different soil. Fail (though this was expected, considering the herb only grows in one location in all of Wakanda). I even tried to figure out what caused the plant death in the first place. Another fail. All I know now that I wasn't sure of before is that the molecular structure of the herb is drastically altered by whatever kills it. The wrecked cells are full of holes and look like they've grown thorns. I've never seen anything like it.

As I said when I began this log: This is very bad.

I've lost a day and a half of work on T'Challa's habit, but this also feels Very Important. And then with . . . what I saw (I guess I "saw" it. "Imagined" doesn't feel correct, though I do *wish* it were some vain imagining) . . .

I'm not sure what to do.

Challenge Day is three days hence. For the *best* possible odds, T'Challa needs a more flexible suit (it would also be great to complete and test the CatEyes prototype to see if it can be fitted inside the habit's head covering, but I might have to back-burner that project at the moment). But even *with* a more flexible suit, there is a chance he could see defeat. Which will mean a new Black Panther will need to be able to partake of the heart-shaped herb.

And as much as I would like to ignore the very much unscientific *feelings* and *inklings* inside my head, I can't shake the image of that desert-skinned woman crushing my homeland within her palm. Especially with the phrase *invasion rumors* ping-ponging around from the Taifa Ngao.

Something is terribly wrong.

I hate to admit it, but I think it is time to speak to Mother and T'Challa.

5

MAYDAY

And Mother is furious.

"You *left* the palace UNGUARDED?"

"Well, technically, the *palace* was very well guarded, which—"

"This is not the time to be *clever*, Shuri!" the queen roars.

All things considered, clever *is exactly what it is time to be,* Shuri thinks, but doesn't say.

"I cannot believe you!" Mother turns on the heel of her bejeweled silk slipper and sweeps toward the door of her chamber, the short train of her fuchsia-and-goldenrod over-robe billowing behind her. Not the most appropriate time for the thought, but Shuri remembers passing her hand over that fabric when she and K'Marah were concealment hunting in the royal garment repository. She'd skipped over this particular vestment because running in the thing would've been impossible. So impractical, Mother's clothing.

"Sneaking out like some . . . common American teenager!" the queen continues to no one in particular.

"Mother, where are you *going*? Did you not hear the rest of what I sa—?"

"We are *going* to speak with the *king*. Come now."

As Shuri jogs to catch up, she hears her mother mutter, "I should confiscate her Kimoyo devices. That'll teach her a lesson."

As the queen and princess pass into the hallway, Okoye and Nakia, both gorgeously clad in their traditional attire, fall into line on either side, and slightly in front, of the two royals.

Which just sets mother off on another tear.

"And you dragged poor K'Marah off into your shenanigans."

Shuri opens her mouth to dispute Mother's incorrect (and fairly offensive—who does she think her daughter is?) assumption, but then she sees their Dora Milaje escorts exchange a glance. And that's when it occurs to the princess how much trouble K'Marah will be in if her trainers knew leaving the palace with the princess had been *her* idea. So she swallows it down. Especially considering how blatantly she's been avoiding the other girl. Shuri's gotten a series of *SOS!* alerts from her "friend" on both her Kimoyo card *and* bracelet, but the thought of adding a K'Marah problem to everything else going on?

No way.

Speaking of which . . .

"Mother, I know you are upset with me, but I received a message from Priest Kufihli just an hour ago. At the rate the plants are dying, there literally won't be any left alive come Challenge Day. If a new Black Panther needs to partake—"

"Are you suggesting that your brother will *lose*?" The queen glares at Shuri so fiercely, the princess feels her face might burst into flame.

"No, no. Not at all—"

"Then cease the dramatics. This matter can wait until the Challenge is finished."

"But it *can't*, Mother. That is what I'm trying to tell you!" They turn left to head up the long hallway that leads to the throne room. "The heart-shaped herb has been imbuing the ruler and protector of our country with superhuman senses and speed and catlike agility and flexibility since the very creation of the mantle! This is an issue of national security!"

Now the queen rounds on the princess, her face alight with rage. "I am fully aware of what the herb *is* and *does*, Shuri. However, no matter how dire *you* perceive this issue to be, there is no excuse for your behavior. Especially not now, with Challenge Day impending and other matters pressing down on us!"

Shuri's skin goes as cold as it did when she was standing beside the bonfire. The drought woman's face arises unbidden and swims behind Shuri's eyes. "Other matters?" she says to Mother, unable to keep the edge from her voice. "What other matters?"

"None that are any of *your* concern," the queen pronounces in that conversation-shuttering way that only mothers can. "You'll forgive me if I find it difficult to believe that our head priest would confide in you prior to speaking with T'Challa or me were the circumstances as critical as you purport. Whatever is happening with the herb, I'm sure it can wait."

And now they've reached the gilded double doors. Per usual, Shuri rolls her eyes as they slooooooowly open.

The princess's heart *does* lift when she sees her brother inside the space, however. T'Challa is standing at the opposite end of the room in front of the massive floor-to-ceiling windows, looking out over his kingdom with his hands clasped behind his back.

"Mother. Sister," he says without turning around.

He thinks he's so cool, Shuri says inside her head. But it does make her smile.

The Black Panther and reigning king of Wakanda is wearing his signature charcoal tunic and slacks (*Does he own* anything *with color?*), and a pair of brown sandals that are glaringly incongruent with the rest of his outfit. K'Marah would lose her *mind* if she saw.

And at the thought of her personal Dora-in-training—which is a sore reminder of the reason she and Mother are here—the princess's joy oozes out of her like sticky paste from a tube squeezed in the middle.

"T'Challa, I have to talk to you," she says before the queen mother has an opportunity to preempt.

To Shuri's surprise, her brother doesn't toss a smirk over his shoulder at her and say *Oh, is that so?* like he typically would.

He . . . sighs.

And a knot forms in Shuri's stomach.

"Your beloved '*baby sis*,' as you like to call her, snuck out of the palace two eves past and paid a visit to the Sacred Field."

Now T'Challa turns around, eyebrows raised. "Alone?"

Shuri can't tell if he's appalled or awestruck. Perhaps a bit of both? She parts her lips to reply but—

"Oh no, no. She took K'Marah with her," the queen mother continues.

And at this, T'Challa *does* smirk. Unlike Mother, the king and Black Panther does know Shuri well. He also knows K'Marah.

"This is not a laughing matter, T'Challa! They could've been seen! Or injured! Or . . . worse!"

T'Challa schools his features, making his expression grave. "You are correct, Mother," he says, fixing a calculated gaze on the princess. "What you did was unwise, Shuri—"

"And dangerous," the queen says.

"And *dangerous*," T'Challa repeats. But there's a spark of mischief in his eye. "You may leave her with me, Mother. I will talk to her," he says.

And the queen buys it hook, line, and sinker. Which irritates Shuri to no end. Why does T'Challa's word seem to carry so much more weight than hers? "Thank you," Mother says to T'Challa with a nod. Then she cuts her eyes at Shuri. "Perhaps the *princess* is more apt to listen to you."

Who's being dramatic now? Shuri thinks.

The queen mother lifts her majestic chin and sweeps from the room with a flourish, taking Okoye and Nakia with her. T'Challa stands stoic and respectful, watching her back as she goes until the moment the massive doors are pulled closed. "Bast, she is over the top," Shuri says, thinking it safe to drop her guard. But then the king rotates away and walks back to his place at the window without the merest glance in his sister's direction. "She's right, you know," he says. "Leaving the palace without a Dora—an *official* one—at your side is extremely unwise. What were you thinking?"

"*Excuse* me? You who used to spend more time traipsing around the city stirring up trouble than seeing to your princely duties?" *Back when Baba was alive*, she doesn't add.

"*While* seeing to my princely duties." He lifts a finger into the air but still doesn't turn around. "There is a difference."

"The only *difference* is that you were a boy and I am a girl."

At this, T'Challa laughs. "Be sure to tell that to the greatest warriors this country has ever seen: Okoye and Nakia."

"You know what I mean, T'Challa."

Now the king does approach Shuri, putting his big hands on her small shoulders. "I do, little sister. And I am aware of how traditional our mother can be. But you must recognize the importance of propriety, especially as a member of *this* family."

Propriety, propriety, propriety. Shuri is really coming to hate that word.

"Now, while I'm certain K'Marah pulled *you* into this youthful jaunt instead of the other way around as Mother believes, I strongly advise against a repeat offense." He continues staring into her eyes as if to show how *serious* he is. (Tuh.) "For the sake of Mother's sanity."

"The heart-shaped herb is dying, T'Challa," Shuri says. "At an alarming rate."

She releases a breath of relief when his expression morphs to bewilderment. "Huh?"

She knocks his hands away. "I 'snuck out' to retrieve more of the herb for the Panther Habit prototype I've been developing. Something is killing the herb, T'Challa."

"Killing it?"

Shuri nods. "I know Challenge Day is imminent, and you surely have a lot on your mind. But . . . well, if more of the herb is necessary, there won't be any left to utilize by the time the Challenge is over."

"I hope you are not suggesting my defeat, baby sis . . ."

Now Shuri throws her hands into the air. "*Why* is that your and Mother's immediate conclusion? *Think* about it: Yes, you took the herb years ago when you"—she waves a hand up and down, gesturing to T'Challa's . . . T'Challa-ness—"became *you*. And no, there hasn't been a successful challenger, or any challengers at all really, during your tenure as sovereign and guardian of our nation. But all that means is that there are unknown variables." *You bonehead*, Shuri wants to add. "As far as we're aware, no Black Panther has ever had to re-ingest the herb, but what if, Bast forbid, you are mortally wounded and need more of the herb to help you heal? What if as you age you *do* need more?" *What if I have to take over for you and I need the herb?*

"Baba would've mentione—"

"You don't *know* that, T'Challa. There were limits to Baba's knowledge just like there are limits to ours. Besides: You were younger than I am now when he died. He probably didn't tell you everything there was to know."

T'Challa's brow furrows.

"Never in the history of Wakanda have we been without the herb. And yes: What if you *are* bested,

Brother? What will the new king do without the enhanced faculties that give our beloved Black Panther the ability to keep us safe? Mother mentioned that you've considered making our existence known to the rest of the world . . . Won't that mean enemies? Who will protect us if the Black Panther is just a regular guy in a stretchy suit?"

T'Challa's eyes flash with anger—though whether it's at the thought of being overcome, or at their mother for revealing his contemplations he surely shared with her in confidence, Shuri doesn't know.

But then his face shifts, and his eyes go wide. Like something has just occurred to him.

"T'Challa?"

He blinks himself back to his center and shakes his head. Then returns to his post at the window, clearly avoiding Shuri's eyes again.

"What are you not telling me, T'Challa?"

"What would you have me do, Sister?" he asks.

"Huh?"

"About this herb dilemma. What is it that you need from me?"

"Oh." In truth, Shuri hadn't really thought that far. What *does* she need from the king? "Well, I've already begun testing so . . . I guess I could use more time?"

"Time?" he says to the window.

Shuri nods then. "Yes. Can you postpone Challenge Day until I get the problem solved? I also need to finish your su—"

But she stops talking because now T'Challa is looking at her like she's grown an additional head. "Surely you jest, Shuri."

"Uhhh . . ."

"We must never shirk tradition."

Just then, one of the Kimoyo beads on T'Challa's wrist lights up and roars like a panther.

Shuri smacks her forehead. "Really, Brother?"

"Shhh," he says, looking suddenly concerned. The king raises his arm to eye level, and a form Shuri recognizes as W'Kabi, son of the Border Tribe elder, appears in front of T'Challa's face like a specter.

"Your immediate presence is needed at the northwestern outpost, my king. We have . . ." The image flickers. "There is . . . something you need to see."

"I shall be there momentarily," T'Challa says. The call ends, and Shuri watches as he shifts to another bead, rubs, twists, and taps it twice, then turns back to the window and slides his thumb over an invisible seam. The pane rises from the floor to right above T'Challa's head, stopping as a sleek, obsidian jet-craft appears outside.

"I have to run," T'Challa says as he steps off the window ledge onto the front of the aircraft. The rounded glass of the pilot capsule slides back the moment his foot makes contact.

Which normally would make Shuri smile—she designed the thing.

But right now, she's too shaken. "So what am I supposed to do?" she shouts over the wind. The vessel moves silently due to its Vibranium composition, but as it hovers she can hear the gentle buzz of the engine.

"Finish my new suit!" T'Challa calls back. As he settles into the seat, an older version of the Panther Habit unfolds around him.

"I mean about the *herb*!"

"I'll have it taken care of!" he shouts. "You mustn't forget: Some of the best and brightest minds on Earth reside within our borders!"

"But, T'Challa—!"

"Finish the new habit, all right? I'll handle the rest." Right before the mask overtakes his face, he winks at her. "Together, there is nothing we cannot do!"

TO BE CONTINUED.

Photo by Rachel Moron

NIC STONE is the *New York Times* bestselling author of the novels *Dear Martin* and *Odd One Out*. She was born and raised in a suburb of Atlanta, Georgia, and the only thing she loves more than an adventure is a good story about one. After graduating from Spelman College, she worked extensively in teen mentoring and lived in Israel for a few years before returning to the United States to write full-time. Having grown up with a wide range of cultures, religions, and backgrounds, she strives to bring diverse voices and stories into her work. Learn more at nicstone.info.

COLLECT THEM ALL!

Set of 4 Hardcover Books ISBN: 978-1-5321-4772-2

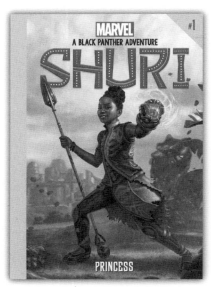

Hardcover Book ISBN
978-1-5321-4773-9

Hardcover Book ISBN
978-1-5321-4774-6

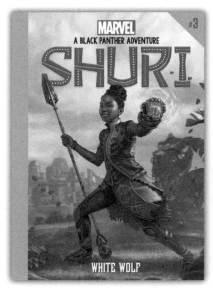

Hardcover Book ISBN
978-1-5321-4775-3

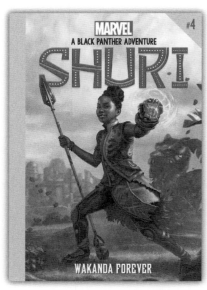

Hardcover Book ISBN
978-1-5321-4776-0